Snake-Killer Bird

Marilyn Komechak
Dec. 2003

MARILYN GILBERT KOMECHAK
ILLUSTRATIONS BY JASON C. ECKHARDT

EAKIN PRESS  Austin, Texas

FIRST EDITION
Copyright © 2003
By Marilyn Gilbert Komechak
Published in the United States of America
By Eakin Press
A Division of Sunbelt Media, Inc.
P.O. Drawer 90159 ☐ Austin, Texas 78709-0159
email: sales@eakinpress.com
☐ website: www.eakinpress.com ☐
ALL RIGHTS RESERVED.
1 2 3 4 5 6 7 8 9
1-57168-770-X

Library of Congress Cataloging-in-Publication Data
Komechak, Marilyn Gilbert
    Paisano Pete : snake-killer bird / by Marilyn Gilbert Komechak.–
1st ed.
        p. cm.
    Summary: After doing a science project studying and videotaping
the activities of a roadrunner, Kelly finds herself the protector of his
chick, a rare white roadrunner she calls Starlight.
    ISBN 1-57168-770-X
    [1. Human-animal relationships–Fiction. 2. Roadrunner–Fiction.
3. Desert animals–Fiction. 4. Science projects–Fiction. 5.
Texas–Fiction.] I. Title
PZ7.K83475Pai 2003
[Fic]–dc21   2002156392

This one is for grandsons
Matthew and Russel
and
grandnieces
Taylor and Jordan

Contents

1. A Fight on the Road   1
2. Paisano Pete Makes Tracks   8
3. Paisano Pete: The Hunted   15
4. Paisano Pete Takes a Vacation 22
5. Paisano Pete Meets His Match 28
6. A Family of Cuckoos   36
7. Range War on Roadrunner Ranch 43
8. A Night Watchman at the Hen House 50
9. A Buddy's Gift   55
10. Back to Mexico for a Rattlesnake Roundup 58
11. A Night without Starlight   69
12. The Star Attraction   77
13. The Ghost Runner   87
Fast Facts about Roadrunners 95
Words to Know   97
Bibliography   99
About the Author   100

Chapter 1

A Fight on the Road

The red sun was sinking, and shadows crept up the dusty road. Pete's long strides left tracks in the dust. He panted through his open beak as he ran. It had been another scorcher in the West Texas desert.

Pete looked up when he heard a roar and saw a truck bouncing down the road toward him. A girl craned her neck through the open window. "Daddy, look—a chicken!"

"Kelly, that is a *paisano,* a roadrunner," her father said. The taillights came on as he slowed to give her a better look. Kelly saw a skinny creature with brown-and-white speckled feathers. Its legs looked blue and strong.

1

"Long ago, Indians painted pictures of road-runners on rocks," the man said to his daughter. The Indians called them war birds, snake-eaters, or medicine birds. But in Mexico people call them *paisanos*. It means 'friend,' or buddy, because the bird kills poisonous snakes."

Pete didn't slow down as he whizzed along the road. He was curious about people, but he didn't like being called a chicken. After all, he was a good athlete. Any other time he would have raced the truck to show them what he could do.

Now, though, Pete wanted to get back to his roost by the river. He had hunted for food all day long and he was hot and tired. If only he could have a drink of water. He could almost feel the liquid trickling down his throat.

Suddenly Pete skidded to a stop, kicking up dust. His sharp eyes saw a snake lying in the road like a shadow. It was a rattlesnake, coiled and ready to fight. Pete shuffled his toes, stirring up more dust. The two predators watched each other. The rattler's eyes glistened in a deadly stare. Its head swayed back and forth. *BZZZ—BZZZ—BZZZ* rattled its tail in warning.

But Pete didn't back off. He had fought rattlesnakes before. Instead, he faked an attack. With a hop-flap, he jumped above the snake's

head, spreading his wings in the air. The rattler was quick, but Pete was quicker. The poisonous fangs struck only the thin, dusty air. A battle of strike and counterstrike began. Quick moves and quicker wits helped Pete avoid the snake's fangs.

That old rattler acts like he owns this road, Pete thought. *Well, he'd better think again!* Pete struck at the snake's triangular head. Again and again he struck with his great beak.

Kelly looked back through the truck window. She saw a swirl of feathers, fangs, and beak. Tomorrow she would tell her friends about the courageous bird.

Soon, Pete tossed the reptile into the air. Catching it, he slammed it onto a rock. With a twisting motion, he looped the snake over his beak. Then he trotted off toward home. The tasty snake was too big to eat all at once. He ate his evening snack an inch at a time.

Pete got back to his roost after the sun had set. He took a nice long drink from the river, then nestled safely in his familiar mesquite tree. Its sharp needles would protect him. In the dark, Pete closed his tired eyes. But they opened again when a coyote howled over on the next ridge.

Pete kept his sleepy eyes focused on the animal. Coyotes were not to be trusted. That went double for bobcats.

Pete pressed himself deeper into the tree branches and looked up at the stars. The only other light came from a house in the distance. He recalled the girl in the truck. Chicken, indeed! Later, when all was quiet in the desert, Pete closed his eyes and slept.

In the house, Kelly got into bed. She told her mother about seeing the bird on the river road. "I still think he looked a lot like a chicken," she said and told how the roadrunner walked like a clown. "Maybe tomorrow I'll take a walk and hunt the roadrunner with our videocamera. Later I can show the video to my friends." She smiled, closing her blue eyes as she brushed her dark hair back from her forehead, and yawned. The *paisano* had to be out there in the desert, somewhere. Tomorrow she would find him. Soon her eyes closed and she drifted off to sleep.

The next morning, Pete stood up, stretched his wings, and floated down from his roost. The dawn promised another good day of hunting. He quickly scooped up a wolf spider and a grasshopper, gulping them down. Then he ran down to some big boulders by the river. Pete hopped up on one of them, and from the high rock he looked for a lizard. *Oh, what I would give for a nice juicy lizard,* he thought.

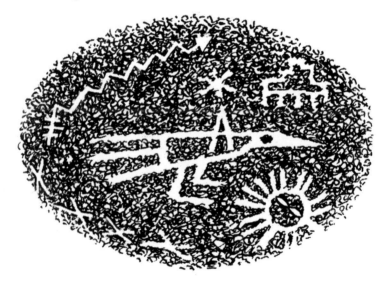

On one of the biggest rocks, near a cave, Pete saw a picture of a bird that looked a lot like him. Long ago, Indians had carved these pictures, or petroglyphs, into the rock. They also carved road-runner tracks into rock and painted them around their sacred places. Because the tracks showed two toes pointing forward and two toes pointing backward, it was thought that they would confuse enemies.

As Pete looked at these pictures, his chest swelled with pride. His ancestors had learned to survive in the desert. Now, because of their adaptability, he, too, was able to live well in the harsh, hot climate.

Chapter 2

Paisano Pete Makes Tracks

Pete walked along letting his wings brush the grasses that lined the edge of the cow path. Brushing the grass forced the insects he was hunting to jump out. Then quick as a wink, Pete caught them on the fly. Today his quickness won him a tasty dragonfly and a beetle. He enjoyed his breakfast, but he was still hungry. A horned toad would hit the spot. Pete really liked lizards best, but so far, he had not been lucky in finding any.

On the path were some deep cow's hoofprints. Pete stepped around them. Once, when he was a baby roadrunner, a cow had accidentally stepped on his tiny brother. The big hoof had squashed the baby bird underfoot. Pete grew sad remembering his brother, but he soon was distracted when a mouse squeaked as it ran under a prickly pear cactus. It dived into a hole in the ground. *I'd better keep my mind on my business,* Pete thought. *I'm burning daylight here. I still haven't finished breakfast.*

Then Pete cocked his head. Something was on the path behind him. *Sounds like human voices,* he thought. *Those are the people who were in the truck yesterday.*

"Dad, look—roadrunner's tracks! See how they weave around the hoofprints? But I can't tell in what direction he's going."

Kelly's dad bent over to look at the tracks and saw the imprint of two toes pointing forward and two toes pointing backward. Some of the tracks were hard to see, as they were mixed up with the cow's tracks. "You're right, Kelly, it's hard to tell the direction he's traveling. But let's go on down this path. If we're quiet, maybe we'll see him hunting for insects and lizards. I think he's come up from the river. I bet he's following this path, brushing out insects."

However, Pete, ever the wary bird, circled around through the desert chaparral. He got behind Kelly and her dad. He was curious about human beings. Still, he would keep his distance. About three yards back he felt safe.

Kelly stopped. From the corner of her eye, she saw something move. She whispered, "He's poking along behind us. If we slowly turn around, I can get his picture with our videocamera."

"Okay," her dad whispered back. "Let's do this: after you turn around, keep walking backward. Otherwise, he will stop, too. He might even run away. You won't be able to see where you're going. I'll walk forward to guide you so you won't fall."

Kelly turned and started videotaping. Walking backward, she wasn't able to hold the camera steady. "This is my chance to get a good video of this astonishing bird, Dad. I only hope he keeps following us down ... or is it up? ... the cow path." Kelly and her dad had to grin at each other. They were making roadrunner tracks!

Pete watched as the two people walked ahead of him. One walked forward and the other walked backward. *Human beings surely do some funny things,* Pete thought. *I wonder what that black thing is the girl is holding?* The black thing whirred softly. But it wasn't a scary sound, so Pete kept tagging along behind the people. They were fun to watch. He caught several delicious dragonflies as he ambled. After a while, Pete ducked into a prickly pear patch. That's when Kelly lost him in her viewfinder. But she'd gotten some good pictures.

"Dad, this is so exciting. I love hunting roadrunners with this videocamera. Let's go home and watch the video on our TV."

Back at the ranch house, Kelly sat with her mom and dad on the couch. She punched a button on the remote control and the video of the roadrunner began. At first the video flickered, and then a roadrunner popped up on their television screen. He looked big as life, sauntering along with his clown walk. He was busy rousting insects out of the underbrush.

His awkward walk was made funnier by the wobbling video. It looked as if he was staggering down the path. They all laughed at the desert clown, but they also saw a lot of details that they hadn't noticed before.

"Oh, he's pretty with the morning light on his feathers," Kelly said. "The sun brings out all the

colors. His feathers are a mixture of black and brown. The breast feathers are tan. His back and tail are black-and-white speckled. There are hints of blue, green, and bronze. But when he is running he's just a dark brown blur."

Her mother pointed out the roadrunner's eye patch. "It is looks like he's wearing makeup! See the white and blue on the outside of each eye? And if you look closely, there's a bright orange dot, too."

Then Kelly had an idea. "Let's drive down by the river road. Maybe he's worked his way up to the place where we saw him yesterday. I want to see just how fast he can run!"

Pete hopped up on a post so he could look in the chaparral for more insects. Suddenly, he heard the truck again.

"There he is, Kelly! Have you got your video-camera ready to record?"

"Yes," said Kelly, "I'm ready!"

"If you wanted to record the *paisano* as he runs, now is your chance. This guy loves to race!" Kelly pushed the record button.

"Okay, Dad, go slow. Let's watch to see if he wants to challenge us to a race."

With a lightning burst of speed, Pete jumped to the road and pulled ahead of the truck. Kelly's dad kept the truck a couple of yards behind. After a while, Pete dashed off into a grasshopper-filled thicket of vines. "Well, there he goes. He's more interested in getting lunch than in sprinting down the road," Kelly's father noted.

"Dad, I think I got our race with Pete on my video. I can't wait to show this to my class at school. I think I'll call it 'Roadrunners Rule!'"

Later, Kelly told her friends what had happened. "The roadrunner—I call him 'Paisano Pete'—leaped down from the post. He spread his wings and floated down to the ground. He looked just like a glider. He sailed down just as smooth as you please.

"Then Pete started running alongside our

truck. It was like he was saying, 'So, you want to race? Well, watch this!' He zipped out in front of us. Each step looked to be about twenty-two inches long. I looked over at the truck's speedometer. Pete was running over fifteen miles per hour!"

Chapter 3

Paisano Pete: The Hunted

After the race with the truck, Pete found himself in big trouble. It had all happened so fast. He was chasing a wren when it flew too high for him to catch. It *tweet-tweet-twittered* at him from a tall barrel cactus.

Whew! This is more work than I can handle. I need a good dust bath. That would feel real good about now. Pete plopped down in the dirt, fluffed out all his feathers, and dusted himself with the fine, sifting soft dirt. *Ahhhhh, dust baths are sooooo relaxing,* he thought.

Pete was about to drift off for a noon nap when he saw a shadow fall over him. He knew instant-

15

ly whose shadow it was. That old red-tailed hawk had been after him for weeks. Pete jumped out of his dust bath and ran for his life.

He ran zigzagging at full speed. Still, the shadow grew darker. He couldn't seem to lose it no matter how he darted about. Pete didn't bother to look up. He knew the hawk was nearly upon him. Its shadow still fell like a black cloud over the ground.

The hawk gave an awful screech, and Pete felt its talons grasp at his back feathers. In that moment, Pete called upon all his reserve strength.

Using his tail like a ship's rudder, he whipped around. This sharp turn sent Pete skidding around a pincushion cactus and under a rock shelf. He squeezed himself back into the dark hole.

Outside, the air stirred with the beating of great wings. Finally, the dust settled and the shadow of the hawk moved on. Pete crept out of his hiding place. He looked around and breathed a deep sigh. The hawk was only a dot in the sky.

Pete had barely escaped the hawk. He could still feel his heart leaping in his chest. Being able to change direction quickly had kept him alive. He remembered that the man in the truck had said, "That *paisano* can turn on a dime. Saves his hide every time." *It must be true,* he thought.

But that close call sent a shudder through Pete. He stretched his wings and stared off into the distance. He could see the desert heat as it waved and danced. *I'll be more careful in the future,* he promised himself.

After he had calmed down, Pete trotted about in the chaparral. He saw a tarantula spider, caught in some weeds, trying to untangle its legs. Pete kept his sharp eye on it. He watched it march across an open space between two rocks. Still

Pete waited. He didn't want to get a mouthful of "weed salad." Timing was everything.

Poisonous animals weren't poisonous to Pete. He could eat all of them he could hold. As food, they nourished him and gave him energy. Besides, he liked keeping the desert cleared of dangerous animals: scorpions, black widow spiders and tarantulas, pests like rats and mice, and rattlesnakes.

Pete knew that human beings feared rattlesnakes. Once, he saw a horse rear and jump away from one. The rider was dumped onto the ground, and he didn't want anything to do with the rattler, either! He ran right through a cactus patch to get away.

But then, not all human beings liked roadrunners, either. Pete was about to find this out the hard way. A man was pacing the desert with a gun on his shoulder. When he saw Pete he yelled, "Sic 'em, Rip," and great brown dog came crashing through the brush. Barking and howling, he dashed after Pete. The two ran pell-mell down a hill, right into a ravine. Sharp rocks and the sharp needles of desert plants cut at the bird and the dog.

Pete was so scared, the crest on the top of his head stood straight up. *If I'm ever gonna fly it had better be now,* he told himself. He sprang into the air with wings spread.

As always, when Pete was in danger, he stretched his wings and flew. The savage dog couldn't reach him. But pretty soon he had to land. *Ouch!* Pete felt the dog grab a few of his tail feathers.

Then, to Pete's alarm, the man started shoot-

ing. *Blam! Blam!* "See if you can outrun this, you quail-killer!" he shouted at Pete.

Quail-killer? What's he talking about? Well, I do like to get a few quail's eggs now and then. But I never made a serious dent in the number of quails.

About that time, Pete heard a bullet whiz over his head. It slammed into a tall barrel cactus, which exploded into pieces. The sky was filled with what looked like giant green puzzle pieces.

Luckily for Pete, the dog was getting tired. His big tongue was hanging out of his mouth. He was wearing out fast, but Pete, a top-notch runner, had lots of speed left.

Pete looked behind to see the dog limping back to his master. He might have stepped on a dog-pear cactus or cut his foot on a sharp rock.

Pete had lived in the desert all his life. He knew that some people would try to shoot him on sight. They thought Pete and his kind were killing all the game birds. *They shoot quails, and they want to shoot me, too! That's not fair! Why can't they just live and let live? Somebody better tell them roadrunners are protected under state and federal law.* The more Pete thought about it, the madder he got.

But Pete knew that most human beings liked

him. Why, he's been chosen the state bird of New Mexico! And on top of that, he was the mascot for the Texas Folklore Society. Pete strutted a little at the thought.

Then he bent his neck around and tried to straighten the few tail feathers he had left.

That done, he flap-hopped up into a juniper tree. He was pleased by what he saw. The man and the dog had gone back to where they came from.

Pete skittered away from his hiding place and looked up at the clear blue sky. He saw airplanes thundering overhead. He wished he could fly that well! Just for fun, he ran up and down the dry creek beds. He loved running on the desert floor. Thundering planes were to be admired. But in his heart, he preferred being a speed racer.

Chapter 4

Paisano Pete
Takes a Vacation

It took Pete a couple of days to rest up. After all, those were two close calls. He thought about the red-tailed hawk. He dreamed a bad dream about the big dog. This morning, however, he felt back to normal. In fact, Pete felt ready for a new adventure. He shuffled his feet back and forth in the dirt. He had an itch to run.

I think I'll go over the border to Mexico, he mused. *I hear the matadors are exciting to watch. Besides, it is a perfect day for a trip. The sun isn't too hot, and the sky is blue. If I get thirsty I'll take a sip of water from the Rio Grande.*

The bull ring was in a large field outside the village and was surrounded by a high wooden wall. Pete stayed out of sight in the a clump of brown grass. When he heard the crowd cheering, he ran and hopped up on a large rock by the tall fence. From there, Pete flew to the top of the fence.

There in the ring was a black bull pawing the earth. His white horns glistened angrily in the sun. The beast bellowed and snorted. He lowered his head and charged the matador. The matador's red cape rose gracefully in the air like wings. The bull's charge missed completely.

I'm like a matador, Pete thought. *I use my wings like a cape. The next time I meet a rattlesnake, I will swoop, dip, and twirl.* Sitting on top of the fence post, Pete learned a lot as he watched every move of the matador. He was glad he had decided to take a vacation in Mexico. The cheers of the crowd roared past Pete unnoticed until he caught the sound of his name. He cocked his head to one side. The children had stopped playing in the field by the bull ring. They were pointing at him, calling, *"Bravo, paisano! Bravo, paisano!"*

Pete liked children, but he didn't want to be a pet. He loved his life in the desert too much.

When the children came running toward him, he decided his vacation time was up. He hopped down to the ground and stretched his legs out in a ground-eating run.

Pete was only nine inches tall. And he was less than two feet long. Still, he was swift. The children did their best to catch him, but they were no match for the speedy roadrunner. He heard one boy call him a *corre camino*—"it runs the road."

On the return trip, Pete hitched a ride in the bed of a truck. The driver never suspected a roadrunner was traveling with him. The wind was a little strong, but Pete enjoyed the fresh air. As the truck rumbled over a bridge, Pete said, "Goodbye, Mexico—hello, Texas!"

Hopping off the truck, Pete stretched his wings. He was glad to be back on Texas soil. A deer trail was close by, and he headed for it. The path would take him right past his roost. Soon he would be home.

Someday, he thought, *I will take another trip. I want to visit some of my cousins. One lives in Death Valley, and another lives in Big Bend. I'll show them my new moves. I will show them I can fight like a matador!*

Pete slowed to a walk and waved his wings like

the matador's cape, making them rise, fall, and swish. He pretended he was the red cape in the matador's hand. He watched it all in his mind's eye. A diamondback rattler watched, too. Hidden by the side of a rock, the rattler waited for Pete to approach, then struck with full force.

Pete was taken by surprise. Still, his lightning stab hit the diamondback's head. Next he spread his wings like the matador's cape. Rising up, he made pass after pass with his wings. The snake, confused, retreated and tried to hide in the cat-claw and greasewood. But before he could get away, Pete grabbed the snake's head in his scissor-sharp beak. With a quick motion of his neck, Pete cracked the snake like a bullwhip. Tossing the snake into the air, he slammed it down against a rock. Again and again he slammed the snake.

"Body slamming" and "cracking the whip" were two great moves his dad had taught him. And these tactics had always worked well. Now he had added his graceful matador moves. Pete felt stronger and more confident about his fighting style, though he hadn't expected to put them to use so soon!

My new wing passes stunned that old diamondback.

I will keep practicing. The matador has only a cape and sword. But I have my wings, beak, and talons—three great weapons. Still, I will work to improve. Who knows? Someday I might meet a very big, fast, and nasty diamondback! I want be ready.

Cooing happily, Pete sped home through the parched range land. Life was sweet in the desert scrub.

Chapter 5

Paisano Pete
Meets His Match

"The desert is like an ocean. The roadrunner is like a dolphin swimming through the waves," Kelly replied to Mrs. Thomas, her teacher.

"That is a very good example of a metaphor, Kelly," Mrs. Thomas said with a smile.

Mrs. Thomas had been teaching Kelly's class how to write a metaphor.

"A metaphor," she said, "describes something by calling it something else. For example, 'Like a feather, the wind brushed the girl's hair.'"

Soon, Kelly knew how she'd use her metaphor about the roadrunner. It would be a great introduction to her science project. That night, home from school, Kelly announced, "Mom and Dad, I have an idea for my science project. I really liked hunting Pete with a camera. I'm going to include him in my science project."

"Sounds like a good idea," her mother said, "but will Pete stand still long enough to be used as a subject? After all, he is a wild creature and runs free."

"I know, Mom, but I think I know where he hangs out. I think I can find him."

Kelly went to her room and got out a pencil and paper. She wanted to write down a plan. She thought about the questions the kids at school had asked.

"Do roadrunners really go '*meep meep*' or '*beep beep*' like the roadrunner cartoon? Do coyotes really run them down?" And they asked a lot of other questions, too. Kelly had some answers now, but she still scratched her head and fidgeted at her desk. She didn't know how to get started. So, she nibbled on an apple and sipped some milk. Finally, she wrote down a title, "Lifestyle of a Desert Athlete." She scratched that out. She

wrote instead, "Roadrunners Rule!" She knew
she wanted to show how roadrunners really were.

*I will let my camera tell the story. But how can I
make it happen? Roadrunners aren't actors. What can I
do to make Pete act like himself?* she wondered.

This science project might be more difficult
than she had first thought. She would have to do
a number of things to make it work. For starters,
finding Pete again could be a problem. And, after

that, how would she be able to get his attention? He might run away if she got too close. She would be careful. He seemed to know how close she could come.

Then Kelly remembered a toy she had in her closet. She hadn't played with it for a long time. It was a little remote-control dune buggy. The experiment began to take shape in her mind.

The next day, Kelly found a variety of small, brushy desert plants. She stuck them in and around the dune buggy. She nestled a mirror in among the little shrubs and stuck a few bird feathers here and there for camouflage.

Kelly walked down the road with her remote car and camera in a bag. After she had gone some distance, she realized she wasn't going to have any luck finding Pete that day. So, she went back home and worked on the written part of the project.

Each day she wrote down what she had seen in her field journal. On the fourth day she was in luck. There was Pete sitting on a post. He was in the same place Kelly had first seen him. He had one eye on Kelly, and with the other eye he scanned for lizards and insects.

Quietly, Kelly set the car down in an open

space near the road. She turned on her camera. She was afraid the soft whirring sound would scare Pete away. But instead, he cocked his head this way and that. In a moment, he hopped down from his post. Ever curious, he ran over to the road, snapping up, as he ran, a juicy beetle. Kelly knelt down in her place behind a sandy hill. Then she made the camouflaged dune buggy roll forward.

The car moved slowly across the desert terrain. Pete hopped right up with a beetle in his mouth. Kelly had to smile to herself. Pete watched the moving car drag feathers in the dirt. Then he strutted and stroked his own feathers. *Wow,* Kelly thought. *Pete thinks the car is a female roadrunner!*

He moved closer to the dune buggy. When he caught sight of himself in the mirror, with a *coo-coo-coo,* he did a roadrunner song and dance. He put his heart into a series of hop-flaps and fly-runs.

All the while he kept his eye on his "lady friend" the dune buggy. *Coo-coo-coo,* he called to her. He waited for her answer. But she was strangely silent.

Then Pete gave her a gift. He dropped the beetle on the car. But the beetle rolled off onto the ground. What kind of female roadrunner would refuse a juicy beetle? Then Pete knew. This was no female. And if it wasn't ... it must be a male roadrunner. An intruder! His territory was being invaded!

Kelly ran the dune buggy close to Pete. Then she ran it in a zigzag pattern. The crest on Pete's head stood straight up. He threw himself talons first at the mirror on the buggy. *I'll show you,* he thought. *You're toast. I'm going to run you right off my ranch.*

Meanwhile, Kelly was getting it all on her videocamera. Pete, as he leaped again and again at the model, made a *clack* sound by rattling the upper and lower parts of his bill. This sound was one he made when frightened or startled.

Kelly did not hear any *meep meeps or beep beeps* like the cartoon roadrunner. Her video would tell the true story of real roadrunners.

In the video, Kelly's classmates would hear the bird's castanet clicks and clacks for danger, and *coo-coos* for calling mates. And Pete would look clownish at times, his tail wagging as he walked. Still, her friends would see a brave and courageous warrior.

Not wanting to worry Pete any longer, Kelly gathered up her feathered dune buggy. She left some dry cat food pellets for Pete, having thought he might like a treat. She also wanted to reward him for his help. Sure enough, he snapped up the pellets with gusto. Kelly hoped to be able to video Pete again. After all, he was the star of the show.

To Kelly's surprise, Pete followed her down

the road. He kept about eight yards behind her, until she reached her front yard. Then Pete ran off into the sagebrush behind the windmill.

Chapter 6

A Family of Cuckoos

That spring, out by the old windmill, Kelly saw Pete again. The wheel on the windmill turned, *th-kah, th-kah, th-kah ... squeeek.* Water flowed into the tank as a cool March wind blew. Kelly watched Pete take a sip of water from the tank. Next, he hopped down and picked up a twig. Then, branch by branch, Pete hop-flapped into a mesquite tree.

Kelly's eyes widened at what she saw next. About nine feet up in the tree, Pete and a mate were building a cup-shaped nest of tiny sticks. Kelly inched closer. Slowly, she climbed up on a rail fence to watch.

After a few days, she put a step ladder near the tree. But she made no attempt to climb it. After a couple of days had passed, she stood on the ladder. It was her observation post. From there, she could see easily into the nest.

As for Pete, he liked building a nest near the water tank. He saw Kelly on the ladder, but he sensed no harm. Besides, he remembered that she had left food for him that day on the road. He made no clicking sounds to alert his mate of danger. Instead, he cooed. He accepted Kelly as his friend.

Each day Kelly climbed the ladder. Each time she left bits of meat on a limb. It wasn't long before Pete and his mate came to meet her. They took the meat directly from her fingers.

Pete was only worried about one thing. The night before, he had seen a raccoon trying to get into the garbage cans by the house. Pete knew to be on his guard. Raccoons had a big appetite for baby roadrunners.

In the days that followed, Kelly watched as Pete and his mate shared the work of nest building. When the eggs were laid, they would take turns sitting on the nest. And, as Kelly would

soon find out, Pete's part in hatching the eggs was very important.

It was under the windmill light that Kelly saw the first white egg. Over the next two and a half weeks, both parents sat on the nest. But it was always Pete who sat on the nest at night. This was because his body temperature was always the same, even on cold desert nights. Kelly had read about this in a book about roadrunners. This special ability of the male was called *homothermia*.

Kelly read that Pete was of the cuckoo bird family. In her notebook she wrote, "A Family of Cuckoos." She made more notes about the babies.

"The babies don't hatch all at the same time, or on the same day. Now that four of the five eggs have hatched, they fill the saucer-shaped nest. Their little oversized beaks are always open.

"Food! Food!" they seem to say. There are now four 'roadsters' in the clutch.

"Pete usually makes a *hummm* sound when he brings food. At other times he announces a meal with a *ta-ta-Toc*. He is saying, 'Lunch is served!'"

Kelly was amazed at how hard the roadrunner parents worked. They were always busy gathering food for their babies. Kelly made a roadrunner menu. The babies liked lizards best for lunch. But they also ate scorpions, tarantulas, mice, snails, and black widow spiders.

Sometimes the morsel was too big for the infant birds' mouths. Then the adult roadrunners ate the catch themselves. The roadrunner parents worked each day and into the night. Once, Kelly saw Pete catch a low-flying bat near the windmill! But that meal he devoured himself.

By now, Pete's beak was broken and worn in places. Kelly knew this was from striking snakes and lizards on rocks or wood. But all the work got good results. The nest babies were growing bigger and fatter.

Meanwhile, Pete and his mate took turns sitting on the fifth egg. Kelly watched from the ladder. She knew that the first four chicks looked like their parents, but smaller. Their black skin was thinly covered with white, hairlike feathers. Their oversized blue feet looked much too big for their bodies. Before long, Kelly saw a crest sprout on the top of each chick's tiny head.

But something amazing happened a week later. Kelly couldn't believe her eyes. When the fifth chick hatched, she looked like a snowflake. The skin beneath the white feathers was also white. The other chicks were now growing darker feathers. Yet, in the days to come, the last hatchling's feathers never changed. She was a rare white roadrunner!

A white roadrunner couldn't hide itself. The eagle and the coyote would be quick to spot it. It would be an easy target for dogs and hunters! To stay alive, a roadrunner not only had to be fast and strong, it also had to be able to blend into its habitat.

However, Pete's mind was on other responsibilities. He was giving the older chicks survival training. And coaxing them out of the nest was hard.

Pete looked at his oldest chick. He shook his head. Boy, did this kid have a lot to learn! But Pete was only getting started. He hurried to catch a nice collared lizard. He held it out to the chick. *I've got to get him across this open space and into that thicket.* Pete purred enticingly, but the chick was reluctant to go too far from the nest. Pete gave another soft purr. The chick purred back. This time he took a step toward Pete.

My goodness, thought Pete, *this kid is scared silly. I'll go slowly. But I guess that's good. He knows open spaces are dangerous. Just as long as he doesn't let fear get the best of him. I can't hunt food for these kids the rest of my life! They have to learn to do it for themselves.*

Pete backed into the open space. He could see that the chick was hungering after the lizard.

Come and get your lizard, Pete coaxed. Survival training was about learning to move away from the nest and find food—without getting caught!

Finally, Pete got the chick to cross the open space into the thicket. Feeling safe again, the chick jumped in front of him. Then he spread his wings. Now that he was out of danger, he was ready to dine! It was as if he was born with an instinct for survival. *He'll go far in the world,* Pete mused.

Kelly watched as Pete continued the survival training. How could he help the little white roadrunner survive? Unless the chick was lucky, she would be captured like the white owl and the white buffalo. Soon white roadrunners could become extinct. Kelly shuddered at the idea.

Chapter 7

Range War on
Roadrunner Ranch

It soon became clear that Pete ruled the ranch. Or at least the part he thought was his. He fiercely guarded the boundaries of his territory, which Kelly thought of as "Roadrunner Ranch."

Kelly looked out over the desert ranchland. Locusts were swarming everywhere. Pete's family feasted every day. On the acres around the windmill there was plenty of water and food. Times were good. Still, every day, Pete patrolled the boundaries of his ranch. Kelly laughed thinking how if Pete were a person, he would have put up a sign that said, NO TRESPASSING!

She had seen Pete chase off strange birds that came onto Roadrunner Ranch. It wasn't a boundary any human could see. But Pete knew exactly where the edges were. And he saw to it that there were no intruders on his land. Not if *he* could help it!

Kelly was determined to find out just how large Pete's ranch was. She followed him as he set out on sentry duty. She tagged along after him for several days. But it was hard to keep him in sight. She zigzagged through the brush, trailing after him. The rough sagebush tore at her jeans.

Kelly had put down a red peg wherever Pete challenged an intruder. She did the same thing as Pete walked his sentry duty. She counted the yards as she stepped them off. Pete ruled about twenty acres! And he had made the windmill the center of his ranch.

"Watchdog" Pete liked rambling around his ranch. He stayed on the lookout for trespassers. *No siree, I won't allow strangers onto my land. Still, this is a big job.*

Nearing the southern boundary, Pete snapped to attention. Then, in short runs forward, he came upon an intruder, a strange male roadrunner. *What are you doing on my land?* Pete challenged. *Skeedaddle!* he called with a growling whir. He stretched out his neck and whirred again. But the strange bird did not move.

With that, Pete jumped forward, flapping his wings every two or three hops. Then he beat his wings with a very loud pop that sounded like a baseball hitting a catcher's mitt. The strange roadrunner wheeled and put distance between himself and Pete. He kicked up a little cloud of dust as he ran away. Pete drew up short at the boundary's edge and clacked his beak several times for good measure. *Good riddance!*

Pete returned to his hunting, only to be interrupted again. He could hear his mate calling him from the tree by the windmill. *Good gravy,* he thought. *All I do is fight wars and put down trouble. What can it be* now?

He stopped dead in his tracks, surprised. Across the pasture from the windmill, some people were clearing brush and picking up rocks, which they put in a pile. Pete's mate and four of the five chicks watched them work. *I'm going to have to stick closer to home. At least until I get these chicks out of the nest.*

Pete was alarmed when his mate approached the workers. The people stepped back as if startled and stopped their work to turn and watch her.

Oh, no! moaned Pete. *She's getting too close.* She was trying to scare the people away from the nest. They had made friends with the girl, but these people were strangers. Maybe they didn't like roadrunners. And what if there was a mean dog around?

Pete's mate warned the people with a loud *clack-clack* of her bill. "Sounds like she's playing the castanets," one woman said.

What the heck! Go for it, Pete thought. She gave a little *"hoot-hoot"* as a further warning. Then she switched her tail from side to side and kicked. The dust flew. The group stood still, looking at her.

"She must have a nest nearby," a man said.

"I don't know, but watch the crest on her head shoot up and down. And around her eyes are blue, white, and red dots. Let's call her 'Patriotic Lady.'"

"How about 'Blue Ruby'?" another suggested.

Finally someone said, "Let's call her 'Ruby Kicking Shoes.'"

"Yeah! Good name for a great gal." They all agreed. Ruby Kicking Shoes it was!

The people finally turned back to their work, though sometimes they looked over at Ruby. *She is really spunky,* thought Pete.

Pete joined his family near the edge of the construction site. But suddenly Ruby spun about and made a mad dash for the mesquite tree and the nest. The chicks ran panting after her with their beaks wide open.

Pete rushed to catch up with her. He was right there as she flap-hopped up into the mesquite tree. The snow-white baby chick had been left alone. Ruby struck with great force and knocked a big, hungry bull snake from the tree. The snake hit the ground hard. A second later it escaped into a hole.

The bull snake wasn't poisonous like the rattlesnake. He didn't have that mean-looking triangular head. However, both birds knew he could swallow the baby "roadster" whole!

Pete remembered the time he and Ruby fought a great diamondback rattler. Double-teaming, they had worked together to circle the serpent. Crouching low, they drooped their wings. They tested the snake to see if he'd strike. Would he lunge for the feathery targets?

The snake was soon confused. Pete was able to find an opening and attacked first. It was all over for the rattler. *Good-bye and good riddance to you,* Pete whirred. He had felt the feathers on his breast swell. *We're a great team,* he had cooed to Ruby.

During spring, Pete and Ruby had great luck scaring up food for the chicks. Kelly's meat treats and the windmill water provided a real haven for the roadrunners. That spring was also a bountiful season for bugs.

Roadrunner Ranch was full of food for the birds. Kelly wrote down the menu in her journal under the heading "Roadrunner Restaurant": There were collared lizards, whiptailed lizards, horned lizards, grasshoppers, moths, snails, centipedes, scorpions, millipedes, tarantulas, wolf spiders, cutworms, bumblebees, mice, rats, and, of course, snakes of all kinds.

A few times Kelly saw Pete eat fruit. He had knocked the spiny fruit of the tasajillo cactus to the ground. He ate it after rolling it around to break off the spines. Also, she had seen him eat prickly pear apples and a few sumac berries.

Kelly saw how well the roadrunners were suited to the desert. They not only survived but also enjoyed life. She loved their curious, fun-loving personalities.

A Night Watchman at the Hen House

One day Kelly's dad came home with crates carefully stacked in the bed of his truck. Kelly saw a few white feathers fall from the truck and dance about, skimming the grass. There were beautiful white chickens in the crates!

A special house and pen were built for the chickens. Kelly put golden straw in the hens' laying boxes. And every day she gathered the fresh eggs. Also, she put out chicken feed and fresh water for them daily.

Kelly and her family had eggs aplenty for all kinds of cooking and baking. They had eggs to

scramble, fry, boil, and use in cakes and cookies. Kelly liked to see the yellow yolks and pure whites of the eggs as they sizzled in the skillet. Sometimes, her mother whipped the egg whites together with sugar. She heaped the rich meringue on top of chocolate pies.

Then one day it all changed. When Kelly went out to gather the eggs, she found most of the nest boxes empty. Someone else had been there before her and had taken all those wonderful fresh eggs!

The chickens were a sorry sight. They didn't cluck and preen. Instead they bunched together nervously in a corner. Kelly worried that they might smother one another. In fact, she was so worried about the chickens that she forgot about the roadrunners. As she stepped out the door of the chicken house, she noticed a hole over by the horse tank. A rattler! Rattlesnakes loved eggs. They could gulp them down whole. This one had a home close to the hen house, and like a thief in the night, he had been stealing the chickens' eggs. No wonder the birds were terrified!

That night at dinner her father had told a story about a donkey that baby-sat goats. "Yes, when I was a boy we had a Jenny—that's what we called a female donkey. At that time on the ranch, we had a big problem. The coyotes and mountain lions came and ate our goats and sheep! Someone had to stay up all night with the animals. That was the only way to keep them safe. Finally, one day, a Jenny got in with the goats. It was too late in the evening to try to get her back in the corral. So we let her stay. Well, let me tell you, I will never forget how that donkey kicked the fire out of one sly old coyote! It was truly an amazing sight. You could hear him yapping all the way back to where he came from. We didn't have to sit up all night with the goats or the sheep after that. We just kept the Jenny there, and everyone was happy."

Kelly had heard about ranchers keeping a donkey in with smaller animals for protection. Mountain lions, wolves, and coyotes stayed clear of donkeys. Their sharp hooves could strike a deadly blow. Jennys had saved many a goat and sheep.

That story gave Kelly a great idea. She thought about Pete and his family. The white roadrunner, Starlight, had finished her survival training. Pete had worked longer with her than with the other chicks. He knew she would need it. Her survival in the desert would depend on being quick-witted. Starlight would have to outrun, outthink, and outdodge many wily predators.

But now, inspired by her dad's story, Kelly thought of a plan. Starlight would be safer if she stayed with the chickens. Also, the roadrunner could kill snakes and mice that frightened the hens. She would be a feathery target to the rattlesnake. Then, with all her quickness and speed, she could dart in for the kill.

The plan just might work. Tomorrow she would talk to her parents. Starlight could be to the chickens what a Jenny was to goats and sheep!

Sure enough, with Starlight in place, the nest boxes soon filled again with beautiful white eggs!

Now, with the egg problem solved, Kelly went out to see the roadrunner babies. She took her field study notebook with her. But when she got to the nest, to her surprise, it was empty. There wasn't a roadrunner in sight.

Of course, she knew where Starlight was. Her brothers and sisters evidently had left for the desert. No doubt, they were making their own way in life now. Pete and his mate were gone, too. Kelly walked back home, dragging her feet a little in the dust. She leaned on the truck. Her throat felt tight, and she batted her eyes against tears. *I really miss Pete and his family. But I will always have my videos and pictures of him,* she thought. She smiled, remembering his funny walk.

Then her heart jumped. She was sure she had heard a *coo-coo.* Then it came again, louder: *coo-coo.* Kelly looked up. At that moment, Pete jumped into the open window of the truck.

Chapter 9

A Buddy's Gift

Kelly straightened up and gulped. The knot in her throat magically disappeared. Pete was right at her shoulder. This was the closest he had ever come to her. "Well, good to see you again, Pete. I thought you were gone forever," she told him.

Pete had something in his mouth. It was a bit of red string. *He wants me to have it,* thought Kelly. "Oh, how nice of you," she said as she reached for the string. "Thank you very much, Pete. You're a good buddy."

Kelly laughed softly as she took the string. Then Pete hopped away. A few minutes later, he came back with something else. It was a shiny ring. Kelly supposed it was from a soft drink can. "Hey, thanks for that, too," she told him happily. *I think Pete has mistaken me for one of his own kind,* she thought. *I am honored!*

About that time, Kelly's dad came around the corner on their four-wheeler. He often rode on it around the ranch. It helped him get from place to place. "Want to take a ride?" he called. Kelly put the string and the shiny ring into her pocket. Pete cocked his head and looked at her. "I put your gifts in my pocket for safekeeping," she reassured him.

Then Kelly ran to climb onto the four-wheeler. As she hopped on behind her dad, she looked back. There was Pete running along behind them. "Hop up here on the back of my seat," she called to him. "Come on, Pete—you can do it!"

Pete gave several flap-hops and came to rest on the edge of the seat. They rode merrily along together. Finally, Pete jumped off. Above the sound of the motor Kelly yelled, "I know. We're going too slow for you!"

Pete had no trouble running alongside the lumbering four-wheeler. Then, in a burst of speed, he darted ahead of them and began leading them down the road. After a while, he sped off into the brushy roadside.

"Good-bye, Paisano Pete! See you again soon, buddy!" she called. And Kelly knew she would. That night she taped the red string and the shiny ring from the soft drink can onto a page in her notebook.

Chapter 10

Back to Mexico for a Rattlesnake Roundup

After hopping off the four-wheeler, Pete found Ruby Kicking Shoes. They headed straight for Mexico, running like the wind with their tails held out straight as arrows. Now that their chicks were independent, Pete and Ruby were free to travel. And Pete had gotten word of trouble in Mexico. They had to get there *pronto*.

A den full of rattlers had moved in near a water well located at a crossing near the Rio Grande. An old well had gone dry. With water so scarce, the people of the village of Santa Rosita had to carry water from a well far away. This was hard work,

but they had to carry it or die of thirst. Then one day the people decided they must do something else. Their backs and shoulders were hurting.

The people of Santa Rosita built a new well near the river road. It sat under a big willow tree. But this was before they knew about the snakes.

There had been very little rain that year, so the land was dry and dusty. The rattlers were thirsty, so they had crawled out of the hills to live in a cave near the new well. The rattlesnakes loved to drink from the little puddles around the well and to coil up on the cool, moist earth. Some of them climbed onto the limbs of the tree for shade and to hunt insects. All in all, they were having a wonderful life.

When the people finished building the new well, they planned a *fiesta,* a celebration. They wanted to express their joy in having a new well. They gathered at the edge of their village and sang and danced their thanks for having plenty of cool water again. The new well was just a short walk from the village, so the people no longer had to carry the heavy water over the hills.

But suddenly something brought the *fiesta* to a halt.

"What is it? What is it?" the people in the back asked those in front. What they saw made them stare in wonder. Dozens of rattlesnakes surrounded the new well. "Where did these rattlesnakes come from?" they asked.

As the people crept closer, the rattlers *buzzzzed* and shook their tails angrily. Here was Santa Rosita's new well. But the people couldn't get near the water!

At that moment, Pete and Ruby arrived on the scene, skidding to a stop. Ruby looked at Pete. Pete looked back at Ruby. They both recalled an earlier time—the day they double-teamed to kill the giant diamondback rattler.

Pete thought, too, about the day he first saw Kelly. That was the day he had the fight on the road. That big old rattler had a bad attitude! And now here were dozens of rattlers with attitude!

Pete watched as the people in the village

backed away, and he grew hopping mad. He jumped up and down flinging dust. Those snakes didn't own that well. Not any more than that snake on the road had owned the road.

"Well, we're outnumbered, that's for sure. But we can't just stand here, Ruby. Besides, I'm feeling a mighty big thirst coming on." Then Pete had an idea. The idea became a battle plan. He told Ruby, "You've heard of a roundup, haven't you? Well, hang on, because we're going to have our own rattlesnake roundup. A little different, but something like the one in Sweetwater, Texas." Pete scratched the ground, then looked at Ruby. "My plan will work—if we're careful. Here's what we'll do:

"You're not called Ruby Kicking Shoes for nothing. You go in and run circles around them—around the snakes, around the well. Take off running fast. But while you run, kick up all the dust you can.

"Now, those rattlers are going to try to strike at you. But they won't be able to see for the cloud of dust. When they *do* stick their heads out of the dust, *I'll* strike 'em like lightning! Smack on top of the head!

"Remember, fast, furious, and *lots of dust!* Okay, Ruby, let's go!"

Meanwhile, back on the Texas side of the river, Kelly was working with Starlight. Kelly wanted Starlight to come when she was called. First she would call her name: "Starlight, Starlight." Then Kelly would make a special sound that was like a word, one a roadrunner understood. Kelly had discovered it by listening to Pete and Ruby. When the two birds were with their babies, they made a certain sound, which Kelly practiced until she could sound almost like them.

Kelly knew that the roadrunners made sixteen different sounds. Some of these she had caught on her tape recorder when the roadrunners were raising their babies. Most often she heard coos, hoots, clucks, whines, hums, and pops. So, when she left a food tidbit at the nest, she would make the popping sound. She did this by smacking her tongue on the roof of her mouth. *Ta-ta-tock. Ta-ta-tock.*

Now Kelly gave the signal when she was trying to find Starlight. And the bird almost always answered with the same sound, *ta-ta-tock.* It wouldn't be long before Starlight was running to her.

Kelly was proud of Starlight. She had learned to come when called. Before long, when Kelly called her from the front porch, Starlight would come zipping into view. If Starlight was penned with the chickens, she would run up and down the wire fence, looking for Kelly.

Kelly and Starlight became fast friends. The roadrunner perched on Kelly's shoulder. Sometimes she snuggled into her hair to nap. Kelly even took Starlight into town when she went shopping. People stopped and stared.

"Can you imagine that?" they'd say, pointing. "A *white* roadrunner—and it's following her like a pet dog!"

The only problem was, sometimes an actual dog tried to catch Starlight. But Kelly was always on the watch and protected her. She would put Starlight safely on her shoulder. "Shoo dog, shoo dog," she'd say in a firm voice. After that, they continued strolling along past shops.

Kelly also liked to take Starlight for a ride with them in the truck. Sometimes the bird would run along in front of the truck. Kelly would yell, "Go, Star, go!" And Starlight would zoom along even faster, until she looked like a shooting star.

One afternoon, Kelly and her mom and dad stopped at the gas-grocery store. Mrs. Brisco, the owner, said, "You heard about those folks in Santa Rosita, Mexico? They got so many rattlers around their new well, they're about to dry up from thirst. There's a whole den of those vipers." Starlight hopped up on the back of the seat. She cocked her head like she understood.

Kelly noticed other cars and trucks pulling into the station. She saw them fill big yellow plastic cans with water. The cans were stacked against the wall. Kelly said to her parents, "Let's help, too. Let's take some water to the people at Santa Rosita." Kelly's mom and dad looked at each other. "Good idea, Kelly. We'll haul some of the water in our truck."

Mrs. Brisco said, "Use water from my spigot.

That's why I got those big cans. I need help getting water to our friends in Mexico."

Kelly helped her mom and dad fill up six large cans with water. Her dad carried the cans to the truck. As her dad loaded the heavy cans, the truck bounced and jiggled. Kelly thought about the people of Santa Rosita. Hauling water must have been a backbreaking job. Of course, donkeys helped. However, there were only a few of those animals in Santa Rosita.

Just as they loaded the last can, another truck pulled in. Kelly saw it was a Mexican family with a boy and a girl. They began filling some of the cans with water, too. Kelly's father got out of the truck and was talking to the man. Kelly could hear him ask the way to Santa Rosita.

"Kelly, come here. I want you to meet Mr. and Mrs. Morales and their children, Paco and Lita. They're taking water to Santa Rosita, too. They saw Starlight and asked about your 'chicken.'" Her father smiled at Kelly as he spoke.

Kelly turned and called Starlight with a *ta-ta-tock*. Starlight sailed down out of the bed of the truck. She walked her funny walk over to Kelly.

"This is Starlight," Kelly told Paco and Lita. "She is a roadrunner. She's my pet."

Paco and Lita tried to call Starlight the way Kelly did. But they didn't sound the same. It sounded like *tu-tu-tup*. Starlight cocked her head to the side. She looked puzzled. Paco laughed. "We will have to practice. We don't sound much like a real roadrunner." Starlight kicked her feet and walked around in a circle. This made all the children laugh.

"I will lead the way to Santa Rosita," Mr. Morales offered.

"Thank you. That would be good of you. But first," Kelly's mom said, "we need to take these groceries back to our house. Also, we need to put Starlight in with the chickens. She guards the hen house for us. We won't be long."

Mr. Morales said, "We will meet you at the bend in the road. Then you can follow us and together we will take the water to Santa Rosita."

Meanwhile, over the river in Santa Rosita, Pete and Ruby were at work. One of them whipped up a great cloud of dust. And out of that cloud, snakes were falling right and left! The villagers looked on in astonishment. They saw another roadrunner flap up and peck the rattlers on the head. Down went the rattlesnakes, one by one. Round and round Ruby flew. Pete hopped and pecked. Finally, the dust settled. *"Olé, paisano! Olé, pasiano!"* someone shouted. "We've just had our first rattlesnake roundup!"

The people began singing and dancing again, all the way to the well. The villagers filled their buckets with the fresh, cool water. They blessed Pete and Ruby, who had flap-hopped onto the tree branch. Both of them were completely covered with dust.

"Whew! We double-teamed those rattlers, Ruby. What a great day for us. What a great day for Santa Rosita." At that moment, Pete had never felt better.

Then Pete saw two bouncing specks in the distance. He made out two trucks headed their way, loaded with yellow plastic water cans. "More water is coming for the people," he told Ruby. "Now there will be plenty of water to grow vegetable gardens, for flowers, and for the apricot and pecan trees. Our work here is finished."

But Pete and Ruby knew they'd be back if they were needed. After all, they had proven their worth as rattlesnake wranglers.

Chapter 11

A Night without Starlight

Kelly and her mom and dad returned late that night. They had talked all the way home from Santa Rosita.

"I'm glad we could help," her dad said, and her mother nodded her head sleepily. Kelly said, "It *was* a good day! Besides, I got to meet Paco and Lita. We are going to be pen pals. Tomorrow I'll write them a letter. They asked for a picture of Starlight. They say she is rare and beautiful. I will send her picture with my letter."

Kelly thought awhile. "But I'm wondering about something I overheard one of the villagers say. He

69

said that there were two roadrunners that killed the snakes around the well."

"Do you think it was Pete and Ruby Kicking Shoes?" her mother asked. "It's just like Pete to come to their rescue."

"Yes," Kelly replied. "He was always careful about patrolling Roadrunner Ranch. He got rid of predators fast. Though he had enemies, Pete also had many friends. I often saw him visiting the roadrunners' thicket down by the river. Pete had connections."

Getting out of the truck, Kelly walked toward the chicken house. She saw some of the chickens roosting in the willow tree. They often did that, now that Starlight roosted there, too.

Kelly called softly, "Starlight, Starlight." Then she gave the signal, *ta-ta-tock, ta-ta-tock.* But there was no answer. It was hard to see in the dim light. *Where could she be? She's probably among the chickens in the willow tree,* Kelly guessed. *But why she didn't answer me?*

"Starlight, Starlight," she called. She looked high and low, but there was no white roadrunner. She even got on her tiptoes and called *ta-ta-tock* into the willow tree. She waited for the answer.

Still, there was no Starlight. Not a feather, not a peep. Kelly sighed. "Maybe she's out hunting. I'm sure she'll be back by the morning."

It had been a long day. She slept soundly through the starry night.

The next morning, Kelly woke up hungry. She ran down the stairs and into the kitchen. Her mother and father were sitting at the table. She saw worried looks on their faces.

"Kelly, I don't know what to think. But I am concerned," her father said.

"Concerned? About what?" she asked.

"Well, Starlight is missing."

"Oh!" gasped Kelly. "We have to look for her."

Kelly felt tears sting her eyes, but she blinked them away. Now wasn't the time for crying. She had to find Starlight. Kelly tried not to think about what bad things might have happened.

Like a detective, she began searching for clues. She went over and over the day in her mind. She called all the people she knew in town. But no one had seen Starlight. Everywhere she turned there was a blank wall.

Kelly had an idea, though. She would distribute a picture of Starlight. The next day she went to Joe's Print Shop with Starlight's picture.

"Please make fifty copies of this picture," she told Joe. "I want it to be a missing-pet poster."

"Well," Joe said, "I think we can print something you'll like. Tell me about your pet. In the picture it looks kind of like a skinny chicken."

Kelly had to laugh. "No, it is a pure white roadrunner. Her name is Starlight."

"Oh!" said Joe. "I've never seen a roadrunner before. And I've certainly never seen a white one."

Together, Joe and Kelly came up with the poster. There were stars around a border of forward-backward tracks. Joe offered to put one of the posters in his shop window. They went outside and looked at it.

"I hope this will help you find her," he said. "You two were quite a sight to see."

LOST—ONE PET ROADRUNNER
She answers to the name
STARLIGHT
She likes cat food—all kinds. She looks like

a skinny white chicken, but she
can run very fast! If you see her, call
Kelly at 123-555-1001

Kelly asked some of her school friends to post signs on their streets. The man at the newspaper said he'd run an ad for her free. "I know how you loved that bird, Kelly. Maybe she just got a hankering to join the wild ones."

"I thought of that," Kelly told him, "but Starlight wasn't like Pete. I always knew Pete would return to the wild. Especially after the babies were out of the nest. Still, he comes to visit me now and then.

"The other morning, I found a silver ring from a drink can that he left on my doorstep. He sometimes leaves me little gifts when he is out our way. Pete will always be my buddy. No, I can't help but think there's been foul play. Starlight didn't show signs of being ready for the wild."

That evening after supper, Kelly wrote to Paco and Lita about losing Starlight. Kelly sighed and plunked herself down on her bed. She looked out the window at the setting sun. "Are you out there, Starlight?" she said to the stars in the sky. "I'll

keep on looking. I will look until I find out what's happened to you."

Two weeks passed, but there was no word of Starlight. The posters brought in no information at all. Then a letter came from Paco and Lita.

Dear Kelly,
   Thanks for the picture of Starlight. She is one pretty chicken, er, I mean, bird! We are

sad you can't find her. We wanted to help you, but we didn't know how. We didn't know where to look.

But last week our family went to a carnival in Santa Rosita. We loved riding the rides. The Ferris wheel was the best. We could see far into the distance. Also, we could look down from the top of the wheel. That's when Lita spotted the tent of "Wild and Weird Animals."

When we got off the Ferris wheel, we walked over to the tent. We wanted to look at the animals. Kelly, maybe we were seeing things, but there was a rare white bird called *Lucero* (which means "starlight" in Spanish).

The bird walked a wire for a cup of corn at the other end. He was with a rooster and a big white hen. All three were "walking the wire" for food.

The hen wore a red polka-dotted apron. The rooster wore a green bow tie. The skinny bird wore a cowboy hat and had tiny silver spurs strapped to his legs.

Lita and I both said, "That skinny chicken looks like Starlight!" Only that bird was missing some feathers. There were bare spots on its body. No kidding, the bird looked pretty droopy. Not at all like the spunky Starlight.

We tried to talk to the man, but he wouldn't even look at us. We hear the carnival has left town.

We told our dad. He said it was a Baxter and Clink carnival. Kelly, look for it if it comes to Texas. We cannot leave any stones unturned! Write soon.

Your pen pals,
Paco and Lita

Chapter 12

The Star Attraction

Kelly woke up and stretched. She could smell the pancakes cooking. *Mmmm, I hope they are blueberry,* she thought. She went downstairs and walked into the kitchen. Her mom and dad were fixing breakfast. "Good morning, Kelly, how about some blueberry pancakes?" her mom said.

"I love pancakes! You must have read my mind." As she poured the orange juice, she noticed that the kitchen looked cheery but her parents didn't look so happy.

They sat down at the kitchen table. Her dad said, "Kelly, I've been thinking about Starlight. I

don't know where she is. But I think I know what
happened to her."

"Dad, you look worried. Do you think something bad happened?"

"I don't know, Kelly. But we've got to track her
down. You remember when we decided to go to
Santa Rosita? We took Starlight back home to
guard the chickens. Then we went to Santa Rosita
with the water. I had asked our neighbor to take
some of our chickens to a sale barn. There was an
auction where they were sold. He came to get
them while we were gone. I think he got Starlight
mixed in with the chickens. He didn't do it on
purpose. But in a flock of chickens, Starlight was
hard to spot."

Oh, thought Kelly, *roadrunners hate to be mistaken for a chicken.* "Dad, have you talked to our neighbor?"

"No, but we can do that this morning."

"Good," Kelly said, her heart beating a little faster. "Maybe he can tell us who bought our chickens at the sale."

"I'm not sure he can, Kelly. Whoever bought them paid in cash, not by check. So we don't have a name. That is, unless the man who sold them knows."

The neighbor man didn't know who bought the chickens at auction. They sold quickly, he said, almost before he could get a seat. When he was given the money, he returned home.

Next, Kelly and her dad went to the sale barn. Before the next auction started, they told the auctioneer their problem. The man ruffled through the sales records.

"Here is the name of the man who bought your chickens. He signed right on this line. I only wish I could read it."

Kelly stared at the scribbled name. "Looks like chicken scratching to me. I can't make it out, either."

"Nope, there is no way I can make out the name," Kelly's dad agreed.

"I'm afraid I've lost Starlight forever," Kelly said sadly.

Kelly's dad put his arm around her and said to the auctioneer, "Here's my phone number. If you hear anything about a roadrunner, please give us a call."

"Be glad to do it," the man said.

Kelly and her dad drove home in silence. They were both wondering what to do next. There were no more clues. All their leads had gone nowhere.

On Sunday morning Kelly and her dad drove to Mrs. Brisco's to get gas and groceries. As they pulled up to the store, Kelly pointed to a sign in the window and said excitedly, "Dad! Look! Read that poster."

Her dad looked surprised. "Baxter and Clink? Why, that's the very carnival Paco and Lita wrote you about."

"Dad, this is the only clue we have. Let's go to town early before the show starts. That way we can get seats in the front row. "

"Just what do you have in mind?" her dad asked.

That evening, Kelly and her parents made their way into the tent. It was small and dirty, with sawdust on the floor. Metal chairs were set up facing a little stage. On the stage, a thin wire ran between two cages. Outside, they could hear the carnival barker. He twirled his cane, shouting, "Wild and weird animals. Never before seen in captivity. Step right up, ladies and gents. Come one, come all!"

Kelly took a seat on the front row. Her dad stayed outside to watch, in case there was trouble. Kelly glanced around. The seats were quickly filling up.

Finally, the showman closed the tent flap and made his way to the stage. He took a rooster out of a cardboard box, then placed it on the wire. A green bow tie looped low on the rooster's chest.

81

Kelly watched as the rooster walked the tightrope. He was in a hurry to get the corn on the other side. In his rush, he got a toe got caught in the loop of the tie. He flopped wildly trying to stay on the wire. The showman snatched him up using more force than was necessary. He yanked the rooster's toes out of the elastic loop. *Not good with animals*, Kelly thought. She felt sorry for the rooster.

When the rooster made it to the other side, he pecked hungrily at the corn. After only a few kernels, the showman grabbed the food away. Then he stuffed the rooster back in a box.

Next came the hen. She didn't get tangled in her red-and-white polka-dotted apron. But she was pale around her eyes, and her feathers were dirty. She wobbled half-heartedly across the wire.

Then the showman put a skinny bird up on the wire. It was just like Lita and Paco had said in their letter. The bird was wearing a cowboy hat

and had tiny silver spurs strapped to its legs. But Kelly knew without a doubt. It was Starlight!

Starlight started across the wire. She moved much more quickly than the rooster and the hen. Then, as Kelly watched in horror, one of her spurs got caught in the wire. She dangled upside down, her eyes frantic with fear.

Kelly jumped to her feet. She was on the stage in a flash. She gathered Starlight in her arms. The showman threw up his hands in alarm. He started for Kelly.

"Stop right there, sir! This is my roadrunner. I don't know where you got her. But she is going home with me."

"Stop yourself, thief," the man bellowed. "I'll call the sheriff. We'll put a stop your stealing."

Kelly's dad had already called the sheriff. They went inside the tent. "Now, see here," the sheriff said. "Young lady, can you prove that bird is yours?"

"Yes, sir, I can. I will put this bird down between the showman and myself. He can call her. Then I will call her. We will see whose call she answers—who she goes to."

"Sounds fair enough," said the gruff but kindly sheriff. The sheriff had Kelly stand on one side of the stage. Then he walked the purple-faced showman to the other.

"You go first," the sheriff said to the showman. The man sputtered, red-faced, "Come here, chicky, come here, chicky, cluck, cluck, cluck." Starlight didn't move. Not even a feather.

Kelly began to bite her lip. She felt fear prickle down her spine. What if Starlight didn't remember her? What if she had been so badly used that she had lost confidence in Kelly?

"Here, Starlight, here, Starlight," she called. Then she made the popping sound with her tongue, *ta-ta-tock, ta-ta-tock.* Starlight's head came up. Her eyes snapped. She darted to Kelly, flap-hopping up on her shoulder. Kelly stroked her feathers. *Ta-ta-tock,* Starlight said. Going over to the cup, Kelly gave Starlight a handful of corn.

The man, shaking his finger, shrieked, "She can't take my bird." Then to Kelly he bellowed, "You tricked me! That doesn't prove anything. You had better watch it, girl. You can't just walk off with my star attraction!"

Kelly said, "She may be *your* star attraction, but she's *my* Starlight. I'm taking her home."

The sheriff told the man he would have to let

the bird go. "That young lady proved the bird was hers. And if you cause trouble, you will have to answer to me."

"Thank you, sir," Kelly said. "I won't leave the man with nothing. He bought Starlight thinking she was a chicken. I have some money I have saved. It isn't a lot, but I think it will cover the price that he paid for her."

A cheer went up from the crowd.

Chapter 13

The Ghost Runner

The next fall the leaves on the maple tree were turning red. A north wind blew cooler each day. Other changes were happening, too. Starlight had been happy guarding the hen house. Now, though, some days she left to go into the desert.

Kelly understood. She knew that Starlight had heard the "call of the wild." She was obeying her natural instincts. *This is as it should be,* thought Kelly.

Finally, Starlight disappeared altogether. "Mom, Dad, Starlight's gone out on her own for good now. I hope with all my heart that she will be safe. I talked to Mr. Collins, the game warden. He said he'd keep an eye out for her. Said he'd run off any hunters. He told me that there was a new law against killing roadrunners. I hope he's right."

A month later, on a Saturday morning, Kelly was out raking leaves. She heard her mother call her from the porch. "Kelly, there's a call for you from the game warden. He's got some news for you."

Kelly dropped the rake and raced for the house. Mr. Collins knew a lot about animals who lived in the wild. Panting, she reached out for the receiver her mother handed to her.

"Well, Kelly, I thought you'd like to know. There's been a sighting of a white roadrunner. It's been showing up in a rancher's yard. Yesterday it was eating grasshoppers in the cowboy's cow pasture."

"Do you think it's Starlight, Mr. Collins?"

"Could be, Kelly. White roadrunners are rare. This one seems more trusting than most. The cowboy calls it 'the friendly roadrunner.' He says he's lost contact with it. But he hopes it will be back."

Kelly was glad to have news of Starlight. "Thanks, Mr. Collins. I feel better knowing that she's free and unharmed."

The next day, Kelly sent a letter to Paco and Lita. She wrote about what the cowboy had said about the roadrunner.

Dear Paco and Lita,
    It sounds like Starlight is leading a good life. A cowboy told Mr. Collins all about her. He said the roadrunner had made itself at home. She ate cat food and the ranch dog's scraps. The bird stands on top of his tractor. It also hops around on the ranch truck. He said she coo-cooed from the top of his corral fence. Then he told about how she zipped around catching whiptail lizards.

Your friend,
Kelly

The letter they wrote back surprised her.

Dear Kelly,
    We have a mystery in our village. The people here say they've seen a strange creature. They call it "the Ghost Runner." Some people are afraid. Others think the creature

will bring good luck. They say it is swift. It flies like an arrow along the ground. But what's really spooky is it shines like a ghost in the moonlight.

A child saw something rise up from a thicket by the river. It waved something like a cape before the moon. It dipped and dived. It danced. People are wondering if there is a phantom on the loose. Write soon.

Your friends,
Paco and Lita

Dear Paco and Lita,

Tell the children not to be afraid. Tell them it is a white *paisano*. Tell them she is their friend. Let them know the *paisano* keeps dangerous animals from their door. Remind them of the two roadrunners and the snakes at the well.

Your friend,
Kelly

Kelly was so busy in school, spring came before she knew it. Not long after, Mr. Collins called again. "Well!" he fairly shouted into the phone. "Do you know you have raised a legend? People on both sides of the border call her 'the Ghost Runner.' They say the ghost is as swift as an arrow and that she dances by the light of the full moon. But now they know the truth. Their ghost is white, but she's only a harmless road-runner. Now the children have stopped being afraid."

"That's good news, Mr. Collins."

"By the way," he said, "did they tell you *how* they solved the mystery? It was Paco and Lita who found the roadrunner's tracks. They told the villagers the Ghost Runner was really a roadrun-ner. The children and their parents didn't know what to believe, so Paco and Lita took them to see the tracks for themselves. 'See,' they said, 'two toes point forward, two backward.'

"Those are smart kids. Now the villagers keep all the coyotes and bobcats away from the road-runner thicket near the river."

Kelly's voice was cheerful when she said, "Mr. Collins, Starlight returns the favor. She clears cer-tain dangerous animals from their homes and roads. She may be a rare bird, but she is a brave one. It's wonderful Paco and Lita were able to help out. They're good friends I can count on."

Soft spring air fanned the mesquite trees. Kelly had been too busy to notice the beautiful wildflowers, but today she stood at the window, looking into the field at the splashes of red, blues, and yellows. Then she saw a spot of white swaying in the wind. But the flower was moving—a lot. She gasped. *Wow! How cool! That's gotta be Starlight!*

Kelly stood quite still. She stared as the bird perched on the windmill ladder. She was about midway up. It looked as if she had a twig in her mouth.

That was it. Starlight was building a nest in the mesquite tree, the very one in which she was hatched. Kelly was so tickled she laughed out loud.

Kelly ran to the telephone. "Mr. Collins, Starlight's come home to have her babies."

Kelly watched as the nest builders worked. They soon had a home built in the old mesquite tree.

Kelly left little food tidbits on a near branch.

She would say *ta-ta-tock* to Starlight. And the bird would answer. Only now she didn't come running. She was busy getting ready for her babies.

But the biggest surprise came later, after the babies hatched and Starlight and her mate were feeding the hungry birds. Kelly had walked out with a bit of food for the roadrunner family. It was then that she saw the gifts: For her there was a bit of foil from a gum wrapper, a silver ring from a drink can, and a twist of blue yarn. For the babies, there was a delicious bit of lizard.

Kelly knew the gifts for what they were—a friendship offering. She looked around. She didn't see Pete or Ruby. But she knew they were somewhere close by.

"Thanks, Pete. Thanks, Ruby," she called. Kelly waited a minute, then asked, "Where are you?"

On the wind came an answer from the river bottom. Kelly smiled as she heard a soft *Coo-coo, coo-coo*.

Fast Facts
about Roadrunners

1. The roadrunner's scientific name is *Geocoscyx Californianus*. It is a member of the cuckoo bird family, *Cuculidae*.

2. Roadrunners are also known as: chaparral cock, snake-killer, scissorbill, and *paisano*, which means "buddy," "friend," or "countryman."

3. The roadrunner lives in desert scrub brush in the U.S. Southwest and in Mexico.

4. The roadrunner is the state bird of New Mexico.

5. The roadrunner has brown feathers with black streaks and white dots. The male and female look exactly alike.

6. Their eyelids are blue with a touch of white and red.

7. The roadrunner is about two feet long; one foot of that is tail. They are nine inches tall.

8. The bird weighs six to eight ounces.

9. The roadrunner can run up to eighteen miles an

hour. Some have been clocked at twenty miles per hour. They are often seen racing down the road in front of wagons, cars, and trucks.

10. A roadrunner can fly short distances when in danger but likes best to run.

11. The female lays from two to six whitish eggs.

12. Their shallow, cup-shaped nests are made of twigs, sticks, and grass. They nest in small trees, large bushes, and clumps of cactuses. But they only build at a height they can hop-flap up to.

13. They make several sounds: coos, clacks, hums, and whines. They do not say, "meep-meep" like the cartoon character.

14. Their song is: Coo coo-ah. Coo-ah coo-ah.

15. The roadrunner eats mice, lizards, snakes, all kinds of insects, scorpions, hummingbirds, bats, and dragonflies, and a variety of spiders. And, on occasion, berries.

16. The roadrunner scares up lunch by dropping its wings and running through the brush. It eats the bugs "on the fly."

17. Roadrunner personality: a fighter, brave, funny, playful, and fearless.

Words to Know

acre: one acre is 4,840 square feet

arid: baked, bare, dry dusty ground

adaptability: changing to suit the environment or place

ancestors: parent, relative, forefather or foremother

cactus: a desert plant with hard needles, stickers, or thorns

camouflage (kam-uh-flahzh): a covering or colors that blend with the surroundings. A disguise

castanets: loud, clacking musical instruments

caprock: top layer of rock

chaparral (shap-ah-rel): brushy desert land

clutch: a group of baby roadrunners

field study: to go somewhere to learn new things

habitat: range or dwelling place

haven: safe place to live

incubate: keeping eggs warm until they hatch

lizard: a reptile with a scaly body, four legs, and a long tail

matador: a bull fighter

mascot: an animal supposed to bring good luck

observe/observation: notice, view, watch

paisano: friend, countryman, buddy

petroglyphs: a carving or line drawing on rock

predators: an animal that hunts other animals for food

rudder: a wood plate used to steer a boat (The roadrunner's tail is its "rudder")

spiny: a plant with hard needles, stickers, or thorns

talons: claw, hook

terrain: ground, earth, soil, land

zygodactyl: two toes point forward and two toes point backward

Bibliography

Douglas, Virginia. "Roadrunner!: And His Cuckoo Cousins." *Naturegraph,* 1984.

Meinzer, Wyman. *The Resilient Roadrunner.* Texas Parks and Wildlife, Austin, Texas, December 2000.

Meinzer, Wyman. *The Roadrunner.* Texas Tech University Press, Lubbock, Texas, 1993.

Storad, Conrad J. *Lizards for Lunch.* Resort Gifts Unlimited, Tempe, Arizona, 1999.

Wender, Leon, and Claiborne O'Connor. *The Little Brown Roadrunner.* Amador Publishers, Albuquerque, New Mexico, 1992.

Whitson, Martha A. "The Roadrunner: Clown of the Desert," pp. 694-702, *The National Geographic Society,* New York, New York, May 1983.

About the Author

Before working twenty years as a licensed psychologist and therapist in private practice in Fort Worth, Marilyn Gilbert Komechak was on the staff of the FW Child Study Center, and was the Associate Director of the Center for Behavioral Studies at University of North Texas. She holds degrees from Purdue, Texas Christian University, and University of North Texas.

During her time as private practitioner she wrote a self-help book, *Getting Yourself Together,* an edition of which was introduced at the Chicago Book Expo by cdBooks™. A second book, *Morals and Manners for the Millennium,* was presented at the Austin Book Fair.

Marilyn and her husband George live in Fort Worth, Texas. They have two adult children and two grandsons.

Membership in various organizations reflects Marilyn's interests: The Fort Worth Freelance Writers, Fort Worth and Texas Poetry Societies, and Fort Worth Songwriters Association. She has published poetry and short stories in the U.S., Canada, and Europe. Last year her interest in lyric writing resulted in the publication of three songs with two Brazilian co-writers.

Paisano Pete: Snake-Killer Bird is her first children's book.